Magno
Mayhem

Elen Caldecott • **Jonatronix**

OXFORD

UNIVERSITY PRESS

CODE Control Update:

My name is **CODE**. I am the computer that controls **Micro World**. **Team X** and **Mini** are trying to get the **CODE keys** and rescue **Macro Marvel**. I must stop them!

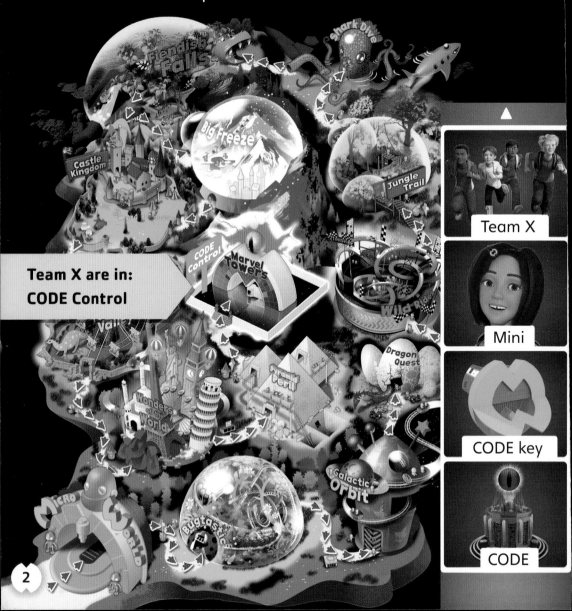

Team X are in:
CODE Control

Team X

Mini

CODE key

CODE

CODE Control cameras

CAMERA 1   ● REC

Team X met a Mega-BITE.

CAMERA 2   ● REC

Tiger was trapped in a web fired by the Mega-BITE.

CAMERA 3   ● REC

Team X tricked the Mega-BITE. It broke apart!

CAMERA 4   ● REC

Max shut the Mega-BITE down.

Status: Team X must now face CODE! > > > >

Before you read

Word alert

Read the words. Remember the sounds you have practised.

jaws   edges   bodies
rumbled   twitched

Suffix spotter

- The highlighted letters are suffixes.
- The suffixes -s, -es and -ies have been added to show these words are plurals (more than one of something).
- The suffix -ed has been added to show these action words (verbs) have already happened (past tense).

What does it mean?

de-activate – switch off

Into the zone

Team X must now defeat CODE?
How do you think they are feeling?

The Central Chamber rumbled. Team X looked up as the roof moved apart. A strange gadget was being lowered into the room.

"What's CODE up to now?" Max whispered.

A robotic voice echoed around the room.
"Magno-collect in position. Countdown
commencing. 10, 9, 8 ..."

Above their heads, the Magno-collect whirred into action.

Cat leapt back as the Dino-BITE's head began to move. It rose clumsily into the air as if it was being pulled up by invisible strings.

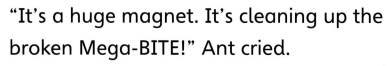

"It's a huge magnet. It's cleaning up the broken Mega-BITE!" Ant cried.

"Surely that's good!" Tiger said.

"No!" Ant replied. "The CODE keys are metal too. We must stop them being sucked up! CODE must not get *any* of them!"

The Ice-BITE's enormous arm suddenly spun upwards. At the centre of the Magno-collect, a trapdoor opened like the jaws of a beast, and the arm flew in. Around the edges of the room, the CODE keys twitched.

"No!" cried Cat, jumping on top of the nearest CODE key. It stopped moving.

Suddenly, Max's right hand shot upwards.
"My power mitts are metal too!" he cried.
His palms quivered for a moment, then he was
pulled off his feet towards the Magno-collect.
"Max!" yelled Cat.
"Save the CODE keys!" Max shouted back.

"I'm going after Max," Tiger said. He got out his bounce boots, but they were made of metal too and were sucked up into the hungry mouth of the Magno-collect.

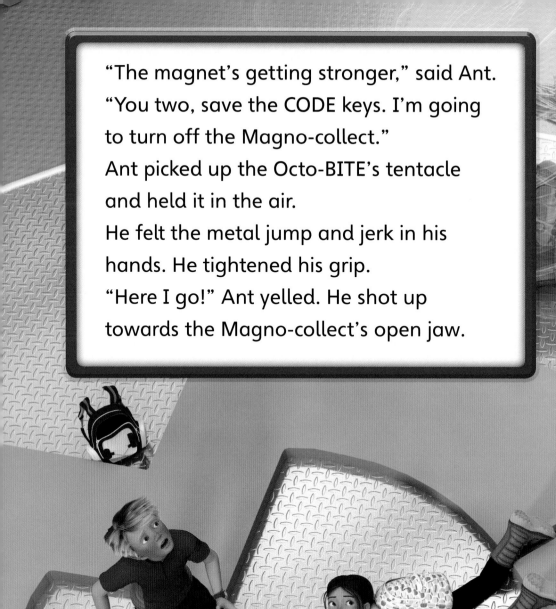

"The magnet's getting stronger," said Ant.
"You two, save the CODE keys. I'm going
to turn off the Magno-collect."
Ant picked up the Octo-BITE's tentacle
and held it in the air.
He felt the metal jump and jerk in his
hands. He tightened his grip.
"Here I go!" Ant yelled. He shot up
towards the Magno-collect's open jaw.

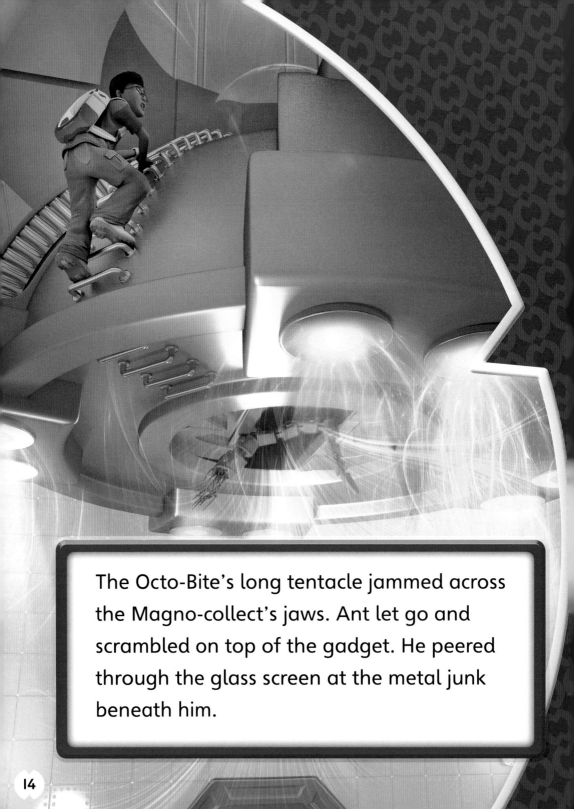

The Octo-Bite's long tentacle jammed across the Magno-collect's jaws. Ant let go and scrambled on top of the gadget. He peered through the glass screen at the metal junk beneath him.

There was Max, his hands pinned to the side of the massive magnet. His force shield shone out as he held off the deadly BITE parts that threatened to crush him. "Hurry, Ant!" shouted Max. "It feels like my force shield is about to break."

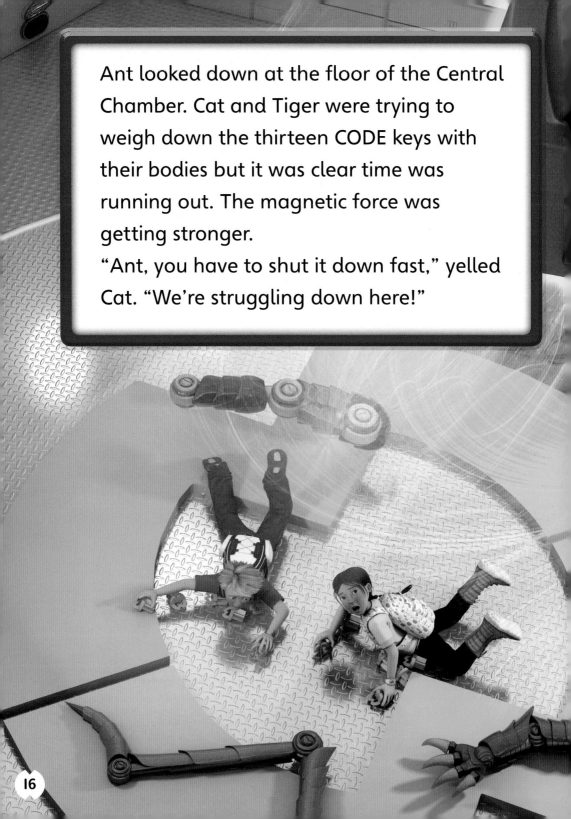

Ant looked down at the floor of the Central Chamber. Cat and Tiger were trying to weigh down the thirteen CODE keys with their bodies but it was clear time was running out. The magnetic force was getting stronger.

"Ant, you have to shut it down fast," yelled Cat. "We're struggling down here!"

Ant had to de-activate the giant magnet, but the controls were hidden deep inside, covered by millions of pieces of metal.
"I need to get in there," thought Ant, looking around. "A vent! If I can get through that I might have a chance."
He quickly shrank.

Ant slipped through the vent and squeezed past the Zapper-BITE's giant head.
He shuddered. "This brings back bad memories."
As he reached the centre of the Magno-collect, he could feel the pull of the magnet growing stronger.

Ant spotted a red button near the back of the Magno-collect.

"That must stop this thing," he whispered. A wall of junk stood between him and the button. There was no way he would reach it when he was so small.

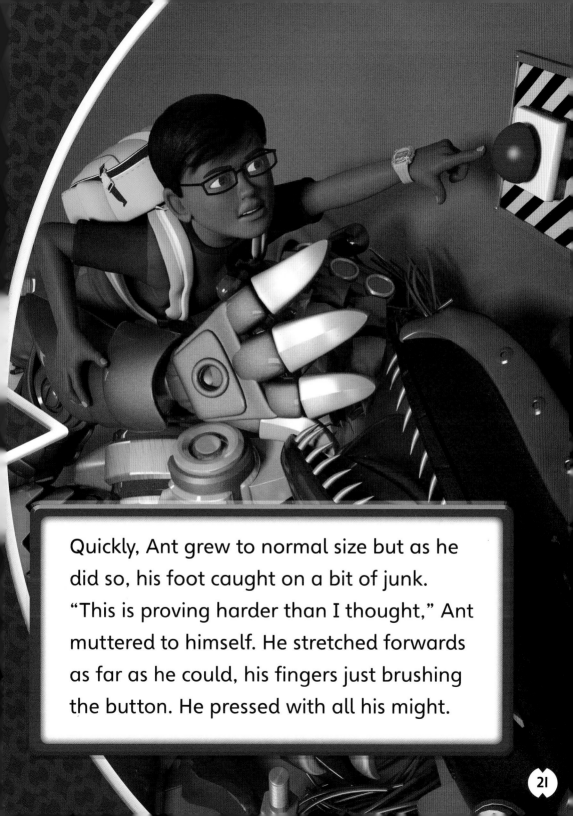

Quickly, Ant grew to normal size but as he did so, his foot caught on a bit of junk. "This is proving harder than I thought," Ant muttered to himself. He stretched forwards as far as he could, his fingers just brushing the button. He pressed with all his might.

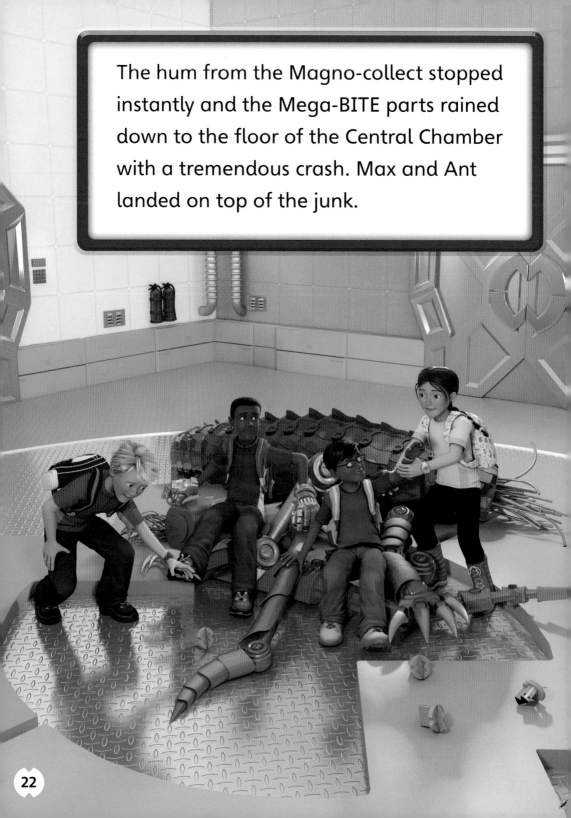

The hum from the Magno-collect stopped instantly and the Mega-BITE parts rained down to the floor of the Central Chamber with a tremendous crash. Max and Ant landed on top of the junk.

"Well done, Ant!" said Cat. "CODE didn't get a single CODE key back!"
"Let's make sure we keep it that way," said Ant, with a grin.

Now you have read ...
Magno Mayhem

Ant's Story

Use the pictures to help you tell the story from Ant's point of view.

Imagine

Read page 15 again. Imagine you are Max, stuck on to the side of the magnet.

What can you see and hear? How do you feel?

Word choice

hungry mouth   open jaw

Why do you think the author chose these words to describe the Magno-collect?

What does it make you think of? How do you feel?